For Brian, Matty, Jayna, M...
You are my everyt...

ISBN: 978-0-578-69214-4
Library of Congress Control Number: 2020908480
Visit www.praisingpages.com for more information.

Note to Parents:

This children's story illustrates the feelings and frustrations of some foster children, and the joy that can be experienced when someone commits to love them forever. It also has a general appeal to small children and their parents who can relate to losing a favorite stuffed toy. Amarylli had a very special bunny, who was often lost, and who was able to help tell this story.

Bunny was lost again? Where was she now?

Bunny was left in many different places all the time. Not because she wasn't loved. It's just that people move around a lot, very fast All people, children, and grown-ups alike make mistakes, and forget. They can be careless.

Bunny was always getting left behind.

How could anyone not see her? She was on a shelf in the grocery store, in the parking lot at the mall, under Auntie's couch, beside the toy box, near the trees in the yard, below the bed, with the dog's toys, and even on the table at the library!

You know, there were times when Bunny was in danger. Bunny could have been hurt!

The world can be
a scary place...
fast cars, puppies,
the washing machine,
cats, shoes,
the bathtub, stairs,
even ceiling fans!
Bunny needed to be
rescued and protected.

Fortunately, someone would always find Bunny no matter where she ended up.

Whenever a new child found
Bunny, they took her home,
but eventually she would be
misplaced or lost and end up
with someone else!
This made Bunny feel
uneasy and afraid.

Bunny loved some of the children that played with her and took care of her in their nice homes.

Sometimes it was hard
for Bunny to get
used to a new home,
a new place to live, and
new people to love.

Often, Bunny thought about what it would be like to stay in the same home. Believe it or not, some other bunnies she knew always stayed in one place.

Some bunnie's she knew
stayed in the same
family's home their
whole lives!
Bunny did not know
what that was like until
she met Amarylli.

One fine day,
Amarylli's Grandma Rosemary
came across Bunny
at her local church.
Someone had dropped Bunny
on a bench and left her
by accident.
Bunny was lost again!
Thankfully, for the last time.

Grandma Rosemary took
Bunny home and gave
her to her dear
granddaughter, Amarylli.
"Thank you Grandma!"
Amarylli was elated!
She had been praying for
a toy that she would
be able to love to pieces.
"I just love this little, soft,
floppy Bunny."

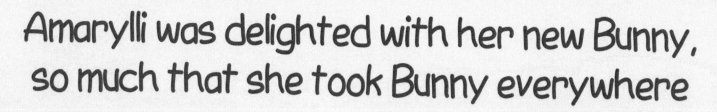

Amarylli was delighted with her new Bunny, so much that she took Bunny everywhere she went ...

in the car,

to school,

out to dinner

and
even on vacation!

Amarylli adored Bunny.
She never left Bunny behind.
Even if she forgot Bunny for a quick second,
she always ran back to get her.
Although Amarylli was just a little girl,
she knew in her heart that love was
about faithfulness and promises.
Amarylli promised Bunny that she would
love her forever. Bunny used to feel lost,
but now she was found.

Made in the USA
Middletown, DE
05 October 2020